THE END OF CHRISTMAS STORY

Alma Denton

Dear Catherine
To the eternal child in us
all. Happy Christmas.
With love —
Alma

MINERVA PRESS
LONDON
MONTREUX   LOS ANGELES   SYDNEY

THE END OF CHRISTMAS
STORY
Copyright © Alma Denton 1997

ISBN 1 86106 571 X

First Published 1997 by
MINERVA PRESS
195 Knightsbridge
London SW7 1RE

Printed in Great Britain for Minerva Press

THE END OF CHRISTMAS STORY

Also published by the same author: *The Kookaburra in the Jacaranda Tree*.

> a marvellously descriptive book, which will take the reader on a journey through time and continents, exploring universal issues of identity and relationships.

> *East Lothian Times*

For Jens

Once upon a time, in a land drenched with snow, a little boy slept all alone in his bed, made from feathers and straw. The little boy slept, deeply and silently, his patchwork blanket pulled over his head to keep out the cold, which otherwise might come pinching his ears.

On his body, which curled comfortably under the bedclothes, he wore a thick red flannel nightshirt that his granny had made for him for Christmas, and had placed under the tree as a surprise on Christmas Day.

As well as the red flannel nightshirt she had also made him a pair of purple bedsocks and, much to his delight, she had sewn a tiny rounded silver bell on each knitted, purple, pointed toe.

Everyone had laughed when Silas unwrapped his bedsocks and they saw the bells tinkling there – shining silver... "ting-a-ling... ting-a-ling... ting-a-ling," they sang.

The father laughed a chuckling sound.

"...'Augh... 'augh... 'augh. Well, Silas."

The mother smiled and echoed the father's chuckle with, "...'Augh... 'augh... 'augh... 'augh. Silas, you *are* a lucky boy!"

Emily, his older sister, pointed to the bedsocks and said, "Oh ho ho ho, Silas! You're not going to wear *those* on your *toes*. You'll wake yourself up! Oh ho ho ho."

Benjamin, his baby brother, from his place sitting at his grandmother's feet, saw the silver bells shining. He tugged at his granny's long dark skirt, hauled himself up, and as soon as he was steady on his feet, he smiled with his two new teeth and walked over to Silas.

Silas held the bedsocks up for Benjamin to see. Benjamin put his plump little hand on the toe of one purple bedsock, tugged it, and promptly put the bell (and the toe of the sock) into his mouth, and out again. He shook the wet bedsock firmly until the little bell rang loudly, clearly...

"Ting-a-ling... ting-a-ling... ting-a-ling," it sang.

Silas looked at his granny who, like Silas, was not laughing. But she was smiling with her deep dark eyes and as Silas looked, her smile went deep inside him and, without a word being spoken, Silas knew her secret. And in that moment it became his secret too.

But now Silas slept in his bed made of feathers and straw. He slept deeply and silently, his patchwork blanket pulled over his head to keep out the cold, which otherwise might come pinching his ears.

While Silas was curled beneath his hooded blanket, the new day was slowly breaking on the ice and snowy stillness outside his shuttered window. As the sun pierced the new earth, the soil beneath the snow grew warm and crumbled. The little furry creatures who lived in the ground in winter smiled in their sleep, rolled over, and smiled some more. The snow above the ground glistened and sparkled and made music even though there was not a sound to be heard. The sap in the conifer stirred, trickled up from the root of the tree and then grew sluggish again.

The ice on top of the stream cracked, and cracked again; some cold water seeped through over the broken and breaking ice. A small robin darted out of the faded rose-hip branch and sipped at the water's edge. His beak and eyes moved quickly. As he dipped his beak, he heard the stream murmur, "Christmas is going, Christmas is going, Christmas is flowing away with me."

The robin puffed out his breast in answer to the stream and flew away. And as he flew he chirped, "Christmas is going, Christmas is going, Christmas is flowing away with stream."

Silas, with his eyes still closed under his patchwork blanket, knew he was awake; even though in his room (and under his blanket) it was still dark. In his waking, he felt sad as he counted all the days since Christmas... Tuesday, Wednesday, Thursday, Friday... he used all of the fingers on each hand, and one more finger for today – Friday. Then, as he moved his feet, he heard the bells on his bedsocks ring.

"Ting-a-ling... ting-a-ling... ting-a-ling." As Silas listened to the bells, a song came into his heart.

"Christmas is going, Christmas is going, Christmas is flowing away with stream."

Although he felt a little better after singing his new song over to himself once or twice, as he jumped out of bed, he realised that he didn't want Christmas to finish at all. It wasn't that he wanted to wrap up all his presents and give them back and start all over again. He simply wanted every day to be Christmas, with more presents, and that lovely feeling when the earth is still and people are happy, especially his family. A time for stories and roasted chestnuts and lots of darkness which made things cosy and friendly and all.

He padded across the floor to open the wooden shutters that covered his windows and, as he walked, the bells on his bedsocks rang again. "Ting-a-ling... ting-a-ling... ting-a-ling," and immediately another song came into his heart.

"Silas, remember. Silas, remember.

This is not November – nor is it December,

But January the fifth – and soon the sixth...

Would you always like things *not* to change?

What might you miss!"

Silas flung his shutters wide open and looked at the new day... January the fifth. He stood on his left foot and shook his right leg. He stood on his right foot and shook his left leg. The bells on each bedsock gave their response.

"Ting-a-ling... ting-a-ling... ting-a-ling

Ting-a-ling... ting-a-ling... ting-a-ling."

Then Silas remembered his granny's secret, which was also his own. Silas' purple bedsocks, with bells on the pointed toes, were magic bedsocks, made by his granny. If he was very careful, and didn't tell anyone about them, each night when Silas slept the bells would work their magic, by singing silent songs to Silas' heart. All his wishes and troubles would melt in sleep, and all that Silas had to do was to remember, each day when he awoke, that he was not alone. Deep in his heart was a little miracle waiting for him, in whichever way he needed help most.

As he looked out of his window, he saw a robin perched on a faded rose-hip branch. Silas felt a little song welling up inside him, so he looked at the robin and sang:

"Christmas is flowing away with stream,

Christmas is flowing away with stream.

But look, robin, look – a camel I see.

Not one camel, robin;

No; one – two – three.

And Kings aloft and crowns on their heads;

They're searching for Mary, and Jesus' bed.

Hi ho, camel! One – two – three!

And hi ho, Kings – your majesties. This way please!

You need a guide, to show you the way?

I'll be with you shortly.

Hi ho, ho hi, hi ho!"